This book is dedicated
to Martha's uncle Geoff
and his flying trousers.

First published in paperback in Great Britain 2012
by Egmont UK Limited
The Yellow Building, 1 Nicholas Road
London W11 4AN

ISBN 978 1 4052 6270 5

1 3 5 7 9 10 8 6 4 2

www.egmont.co.uk

A CIP catalogue record for this title is available from the British Library
Printed and bound by CPI Group (UK) Ltd, Croydon, CR0 4YY

51468/1

Agatha Parrot

and the Zombie Bird

Typed out neatly by

Kjartan Poskitt

Illustrated by David Tazzyman

EGMONT

The gang!

When **Bianca** was little, she planted her welly boots to see if they would grow.

Martha's first ever football was an orange, and her teddy was the goalkeeper.

Agatha (that's me). When I was a baby, I could put my big toe in my nose. And that's true.

Ivy used to pull all her dolls apart, then put them back together with the bits mixed up. Eeek!

Ellie thought she had a pet stick insect, but it was only a stick.

10
8 9
7
5 6
4
2 3
1
10
8 9
7
5 6
4
2 3
1
Odd Street
Primary
School

ODD STREET

No 1
Bianca
No 3
Martha
No 5
Agatha
No 7
Ivy
No 9
Ellie
1
3
5
9
SCHOOL

CONTENTS

Don't Worry, This Book Won't Turn You Into a Frog

Hiya!

I'm Agatha Jane Parrot and guess what this book is all about? MAGIC!

Sounds of spooky music: Ooo-weee-ooo-wooo!

(You have to sing those spooky sounds out loud. Oh, go on! You know you want to.)

I hope you're going to read it all because I've got a friend called Ellie Slippin who won't even look at the cover. She's scared that she'll accidentally read out some magic words and turn herself into a frog or something ha ha!

Oh wow,

wouldn't it be

AWESOME

if that worked

for real? Imagine

you were sitting in

the classroom next

to somebody reading

this book, and *PA-DAFF*

they suddenly turned into a frog! Or maybe an octopus or a sausage or even a little old granny? Wicked!

Sorry. This book can't do that but at least I'm being honest about it.

I hate books where people do spells with magic words, because I can never resist trying them out. I warn you, you can end up looking pretty silly when you're standing on a table waving your ruler at the teacher and waiting for her to turn into a tomato. BORING.

I think if you try out magic words from a book and they don't

work, you should get your money back . . . plus £1,000,000,000 compensation for making you look silly. How about that? I'd be mega rich by now ha ha *KER-CHING!*

The good news is that this book has a magic trick later on that you CAN do. It's called the Pen of Destiny and there's even a clue to show you how it works. What's more, there's also a bit of REAL MAGIC which isn't a trick at all. It's really real!

Time for more spooky music: Ooo-weee-ooo-wooo!

The story starts with something that happened ages ago so first of all we have to get in a time machine and go backwards.

Zum zum zum – PING!

Now let's see where we've ended up . . .

Tiddly Tot Parties

Aw, we were SO cute!

We've gone back to when all of us on Odd Street were just little tiddly tots and we'd just started school. There was me, Ivy, Bianca, Ellie and big jolly Martha who always laughed at everything and still does.

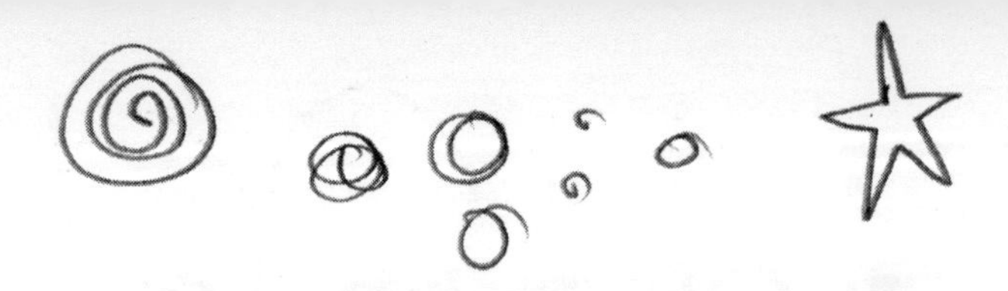

Our houses are the ones by the school gates. Further up the street you get to the shops, and then it's some big posh houses. The biggest poshest house has a tree in front, and that's where Gwendoline Tutt lives.

Nobody knew Gwendoline before we went to school, so after about a week Gwendoline's mum invited us all up for a party. Before that I'd only been to two other parties and they had both been BRILLIANT.

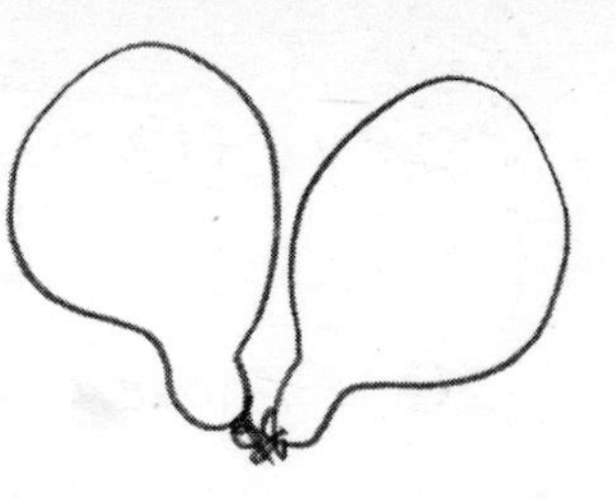

Party number 1

Martha had a pizza party where we started off by . . . *get ready for a big surprise* . . . eating pizzas! Then we played games like 'who can bite their pizza into the funniest shape?' or 'who can get the most pizza crusts sticking out of their mouth?'. Bianca was sick, Ellie split her dress and Martha blew all her candles out with one big burp. WAHEY! We love Martha.

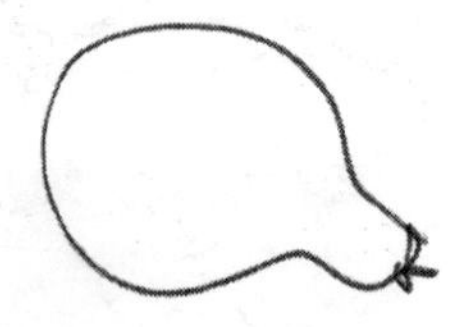

Party number 2

The other party was in Ivy's house. We were all dressed as fairies, so Ivy (who is mad by the way) decided we should do some flying. Ivy showed us how to hold up an umbrella and then jump down all the stairs in one go*, but her mum completely freaked out and shut us in the lounge.

So then Ivy got all the cushions off the sofa and piled them up in the middle. We jumped up and down on them to see if we could get high enough to whack the ceiling light with our magic wands ha ha!* Fun doesn't get better than that. YAHOO! We love Ivy too.

(*The old man who is typing this book for me says I have to tell you NOT TO DO THESE THINGS. Because if you hurt yourself we will not be responsible. In fact we'll LAUGH ha ha it serves you right.)

But party number 3 was Gwendoline's party.

To start with we all turned up in our little party dresses and handed over our presents. Gwendoline just ripped them open and then stuck her hand out and said 'next' after each one. How charming. Then her mum sent us into

their lounge which was **HUGE**. It had a white carpet and a row of kitchen chairs all lined up like in a classroom.

'Sit still and don't touch anything,' she said. 'Gwendoline has a treat for you.'

The treat was a clown with a yellow curly wig and a big red nose called Leggo Laughalot. First he made us do pass the parcel, but every time the music stopped it was

ALWAYS on Gwendoline, so she always took the paper off and in the end she won the prize (sketchbook and crayons). Gwendoline and Leggo both thought it was really funny but we didn't.

Next he did a magic show. He said that anybody who helped him would get a chocolate lolly, so we all kept putting our hands up to volunteer. Guess who he picked EVERY TIME?

In the end he put some music on for a dancing competition. Out of all of us, Bianca was well the best because she'd had lessons since she was a baby. If it wasn't Bianca, it had to be Ivy because she could put her leg up behind her ear, or maybe Ellie because she could do spins without falling over. Even Martha could do some jolly wobbles in time to the music. The only person not trying was Gwendoline who just moaned that she wanted to watch telly. So guess who Leggo made the winner? I'll give you a choice. Was it:

- The pink stuffed dog lying on the windowsill?
- The armchair with a lever on the side to make the back go flat BUT we weren't allowed to play with it?
- Queen Victoria (1837–1901)?
- Gwendoline?

Ooooh . . . who could it be?

Here's a clue. Pick the most unlikely one and that's the answer. Yes that's right, it was Gwendoline so give yourself a round of applause clap clap clap and a big BOOOO to Leggo Laughalot.

Anyway, that's enough about Gwendoline and her rubbish clown, so let's get back into the time machine and forget about it.

Zum zum zum – PING!

Here we are again and it's five

years after Gwendoline's party. The big question is: have you forgotten about that clown? No? Even after five years? Of course you haven't because things like that stick in your mind for EVER.

The Big Announcement

Monday morning at Odd Street School always starts with everybody in the hall for assembly. Tiddlies at the front, biggies at the back, and teachers round the sides so that nobody can escape. Ivy says that one day she's

going to smuggle a spade in and dig an escape tunnel when nobody's looking **ha ha!** She'd just fall into the store room and land on Motley the caretaker having a nice little morning sleep on the gym mats.

We all sing a song with Miss Bunn playing the plinky plonk piano, then Mrs Twelvetrees gives us a serious talk. It's usually something like:

'I don't want to see

any more children throwing their old banana skins at the hall ceiling. Sometimes it's weeks before they get unstuck. Then they can fall on somebody's head and it is NOT funny.'

(Oh no? She's dead wrong there. It's wicked.)

But this story is about one Monday when Mrs T was all of a twitter. Her necklaces were jangling and she'd slapped on about

three tonnes of her reddest lipstick specially.

'I say chaps, I've got splendid news! We've got a special guest coming into school. He's going to perform his new show for us, and if it goes well, he might go on to tour the world!'

Oooooooooh!

Everybody gasped and even the teachers were excited. Little old Miss Bunn said, 'It could be the next Elvis Presley!' and went all giggly. If you haven't heard of Elvis Presley, he was the biggest pop star ever because he used to sing 'I'm all shook up uh-huh-huh!' and then wiggle his bottom a lot. It must have looked a bit like Ivy pulling her tights up but I bet Elvis wasn't as funny.

'I can't tell you who it is yet . . .' said Mrs T.

Angry mutterings from the crowd: WHY NOT? BORING! WE WANT TO KNOW!

'. . . but he might need a volunteer to help him.'

WAM BASH CLATTER!

Miss Bunn was obviously thinking about helping Elvis Presley and had fainted into a pile of stacking chairs. Poor Miss Bunn! But then she sat up with a big dreamy smile on her face, so at least she wasn't *all shook up uh-huh-huh* like Elvis. Ha ha!

The Mystery Van

At playtime we were talking about who we'd want the visitor to be if we could have anybody we wanted. Here's the list with my marks out of ten for brilliance:

Ellie: A fairy princess.

Before you say that Ellie's

a bit soft, have a think about it. When you're having a cheese sandwich for the millionth lunchtime in a row, wouldn't it be FAB if there was a fairy princess handy to turn it into curry and poppadoms? You've got to say YES. (7/10)

Ivy: Julius Caesar and the Romans.

Ivy wants to do what Queen Boudicca did and ride round in a chariot with swords sticking out of the wheels and chop all the Roman soldiers' legs off **ha ha wicked!**

Actually these days you're probably not allowed to use swords. They'd make you use plastic forks from the school kitchen. You'd be lucky if you even managed to make a hole in their tights. Did Roman soldiers wear tights? Hmmm . . . sorry Ivy. (3/10)

Bianca: Noah and his ark.

We'd get two of every animal including pandas and koala bears oh they're **SO cute!** But we'd also get buffaloes and slugs

and rats and warthogs . . .
gosh the school would stink
whiffy pong YUK. (4/10)

Martha: Uncle Geoff.

Super! Martha's uncle Geoff is famous because he used to be a real fatty, but he won slimmer of the year. There was a photo of him in the paper being so skinny that he could fit

himself into one leg of his
old giant trousers **ha ha!**

He wants to win again this year, but if he lost the same kilograms as last year, his weight would be MINUS so he'd float upwards. He could take us flying round in his giant trousers – how wicked would that be? (10/10)

I therefore declared Uncle Geoff the winner. DA-DAH!

So there we were in the

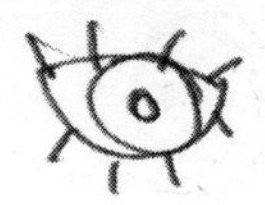

playground having this very serious discussion about soldiers' tights and flying trousers when we were most rudely interrupted. Miss Barking came marching over towards us.

Miss Barking is the deputy headteacher. She's got short black hair and big square glasses like telly screens and she's always bothering people with *issues*. Issues are things that you can worry about if you're bored of being happy. Here are a

few, so if you'd like something to worry about, help yourself:

Have you recycled your yoghurt pot?

Are your socks ecologically friendly?

Has your pencil case got a health and safety warning on it in case a small child tries to climb inside and zip itself up?

Miss B's latest issue was animal welfare, and she'd got Motley to put up a special bird feeder. It was dangling off the bike shed drainpipe, and it had three tubes full of different bird food. She was holding a form to fill in, and had her pen out ready to tick some boxes.

'How many birds have you seen using the feeder?' she asked us.

Eeek! It was a bit embarrassing. Nobody wanted to tell her the truth.

'Oh come along, you must have some idea,' said Miss Barking looking at her form. 'Would you say *over one hundred*?'

'Ummm . . .' we all said.

'All right then. How about *over fifty*?'

'Er . . .'

'*Over twenty-five*?'

'Ah . . .'

'*Over ten?*'

'Eeee . . .' we all said shaking our heads.

'Now come along,' said Miss Barking sounding desperate. 'There must have been a few birds on our feeder. The food level has gone down.'

We hardly liked to tell her that the boys had been getting the seeds and pellets out and pinging them at each other. Plus Martha ate a bit to try it and Bianca used some of the blue blobs to decorate her ruler.

'Shall we say five birds?' asked Miss Barking. 'Or four? Or three . . .'

She was getting closer.

'Two?'

Nearly there.

'One?'

Oooh – just one more guess should do it! Actually I was feeling a bit sorry for her, but then a dirty fat pigeon came flapping down and landed on the feeder.

'Aha! Now watch,' said Miss Barking getting all excited. 'Which tube of food will it go for? There's the high protein pellets, or the seeds for good digestion, or maybe the fat drops for energy. Animals are much cleverer than us, their natural instincts

tell them what is best for them.'

The fat pigeon took one sniff. It then fluttered over to the bin where somebody had chucked an old fried chicken box and got stuck in!

Miss Barking walked off crossly. Obviously her form hadn't got a box to tick saying 'cold chips with barbecue sauce'.

Poor Miss Barking. She's as nutty as her high protein bird pellets, but she means well.

Just then a black van came in through the school gates. It must have been a new person to the school because they parked right outside the main doors on the FORBIDDEN

PLACE. Oh dear!

The forbidden place is a big white square on the ground with zigzags going across it. Nobody's allowed to park there because it's very DANGEROUS. If there was a fire/flood/earthquake/alien invasion/escaped gorilla then anything parked there would block our escape EEEK panic panic. But what makes it even more dangerous is that the forbidden place is

guarded by a fearsome beast who will leap out and breathe fire on you and devour your bones ha ha!

Well actually she won't do that, but I'm talking about Miss Wizzit the school receptionist and she can strike terror into anyone. It's true, she's armed with a stapler and she's ready to use it. NOBODY messes with Miss Wizzit.

Me and Martha and Ivy and Bianca and Ellie went to lean on the

wall and watch. A man with black sunglasses and black skinny jeans got out of his black van. Oh boy, he was going to be for it. Tee hee, we couldn't wait!

He looked round at our lovely school and pulled a face as if it was old and smelly. (Which it is actually, but that wasn't very good manners, was it?) Next, he bent down to admire himself in the van's little sticky-out door mirror. Ivy burst out giggling, so he got cross and stomped up to the main door and gave the button a rude prod.

'Wizzit?' said the voice on the intercom.

'I am Misto the Mysterious,' he said.

'No,' said Miss Wizzit's voice. 'I want your REAL name or you're not coming in.'

'Oh yeah?' said Mr Skinny Jeans. 'Then you can tell your Mrs Twelvetrees that I'm going.'

He got back into his van and so we thought that was the end of that.

BORING.

But suddenly Mrs Twelvetrees came bursting out of the door with all her necklaces and bangles jangling. She hurried over to tap on his van window. There was lots of hand-waving and being sorry, and then the man got out again. Mrs T zoomed in front to hold the school door open and in he went. Gosh, anybody would think that he was somebody posh off the telly or something.

The van was still in the

FORBIDDEN PLACE so me and Martha went for a closer look. The windows at the back were all blacked out so we couldn't see inside, but there was a mark on the glass where a sticker had been peeled off. You could still make out the shape though, and I was sure I recognised it!

'Hey Martha,' I said. 'Remember that party at Gwendoline's house?'

Now here's the good thing about

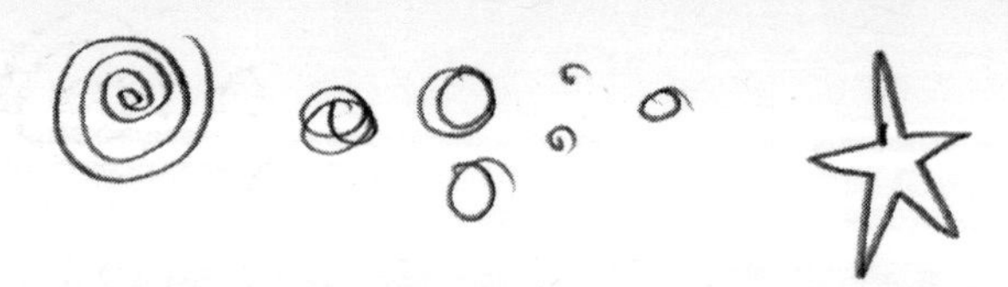

Martha. She never remembers bad stuff, only good stuff. All she said was, 'Five types of jelly!'

'Never mind the jelly. Do you remember the clown?'

'You mean Leggo Laughalot? Who cares about him? There was lime, orange, strawberry . . .'

'YES YES, but remember the clown handed out stickers at the end? They were like a custard pie with a clown face on it.'

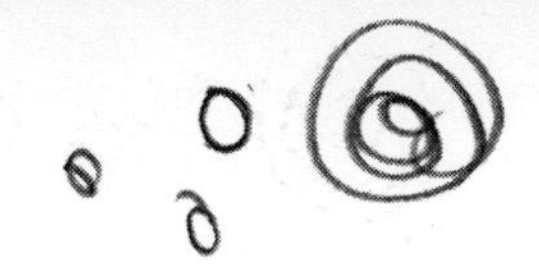

'So?'

'Look at this mark. What do you think?'

Martha had a good look. 'If that was one of Leggo's stickers, what's it doing there?'

'This could be his van,' I said.

'Hmmm,' said Martha thinking hard but then her brain wandered off. 'And lemon. Oh, and number five was blackcurrant! Yummy.'

Bah, useless. But if I was right

about the sticker, did that mean this Misto person was really Leggo Laughalot? I needed to know more about this guy so I went to see Pukey.

Don't worry. You're not supposed to know who Pukey is yet but he comes up next so get ready. Three two one GO . . .

Pukey and the Magic Pencil

Pukey Higginson is a very useful person, because nearly everything in school makes him feel sick. He's always being sent out to sit on one of the waiting seats in the reception area with his head hanging over a bucket. The good thing is that

he sees everything that goes on. He's better than CCTV.

When I got to reception, Pukey was sitting on the far side. Miss Wizzit was sitting behind her big desk staring out of the window at the van parked in the FORBIDDEN PLACE. I thought I could just walk past her but . . .

'Agatha Parrot!' she snapped without looking round. 'Just WHERE do you think YOU'RE going?'

'Just seeing if Thomas is feeling better,' I said. (That's Pukey's real name.)

I thought she'd send me away, but Miss Wizzit just kept staring at the evil van. She wasn't interested in me. Phew!

'Hi Pukey,' I said in a caring and interested way. 'How much sick have you done?'

'Urgh . . . none yet,' said Pukey looking up from his bucket.

'Let me see,' I said.

Pukey and me stuck our heads down in the bucket together so we could have a private chat.

'What did that man want?' I asked him.

'Dunno,' said Pukey pointing a finger at Mrs Twelvetrees's office door. 'She took him straight inside. Mr Twelvetrees was already in there waiting.'

'Hmm . . . interesting,' I said.

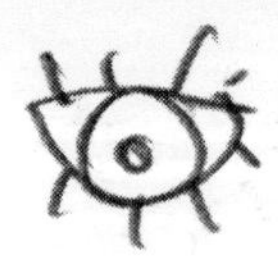

'They must be old friends.'

But I was wrong. The office door opened so we pulled our heads out of the bucket. We saw Mr Twelvetrees stepping out backwards.

'Sorry,' he said to whoever was still inside. 'So sorry. I just thought I could have helped.'

The door shut in his face and he was left standing outside looking a bit sad.

Mr Twelvetrees is married to

Mrs Twelvetrees, but he looks more like her dad. That's because he used to be a headteacher too but now he's just bald and wears grey trousers. He comes in to Odd Street to run drama group and help on things like sports day.

When he saw Pukey looking a bit green, he smiled and came over.

'I see your problem Thomas,' said Mr T then he reached down and pulled a pencil out of Pukey's ear. 'Aha! I was looking for that. Thank you.'

I meant to tell you, Mr T does little magic tricks. We've seen them all before but they're still good. Even Pukey laughed a bit, although he doesn't laugh too much in case any puke comes out.

The office door opened again and Mrs T stuck her head out to speak to Miss Wizzit. 'Could you ask Mr Motley to come and see us?'

'Are you sure I can't help?' offered Mr Twelvetrees.

'Not you,' came a voice from inside.

Mrs T did a big lipsticky smile at all of us then she pulled her head back in and shut her door.

Miss Wizzit made an angry hissing noise and stabbed at a button on her desk. There was a bleeping sound which went on for ages. Motley was obviously not answering his walkie-talkie.

'Shall I go and find Mr Motley?' I asked.

'I suppose you'd better,' said Miss Wizzit which is her grumpy way of saying *how very kind of you to offer, yes please*! 'But he could be anywhere.'

No he couldn't because it was just past eleven o'clock and I knew exactly where he was.

Secrets in the Store Room

Just next to the cloakrooms is a funny old door marked *PRIVATE*. If you go through it, watch out because it's a bit dark and there's some wonky steps going down. At the bottom there's another door which says *WARNING!*

KEEP OUT: DANGER but that's a big lie because it's only the store room.

I went down there and, just as I expected, there was music coming out of the keyhole. I banged on the door and the music snapped off.

'Hello?' I said.

Nothing.

'Mr Motley,' I said, doing my very important voice. 'It's me, Agatha Parrot. I know you're in there.'

'Go away. This is a private staffroom,' said Motley's voice.

'Mrs Twelvetrees wants you.'

'I'm busy.'

'No you're not, you're having a cup of tea and watching your secret telly.'

'That's a bad thing to say. And you're bad too.'

'If you don't let me in then I'll go and tell Miss Wizzit what you're doing. But if you do let me in I want two biscuits and you can have five more minutes of telly. Have we got a deal?'

'Bah!'

The door opened.

'You need to go and talk to a man in Mrs Twelvetrees's office,' I said.

'But I'm sorting out the store room,' said Motley. He always pretends to be grumpy, but he doesn't fool me, especially when he's handing out biscuits. 'I suppose you better take one for Martha too. And one for Bianca, and one for Ellie and . . .'

BOM BOP BOOM

I nearly jumped out of my socks! It was a thuddy noise coming from above us. We were right underneath the school hall where the boys were having football practice. Little bits of dust were coming down from a square shape in the ceiling. Motley saw me looking up at it.

'It's a trapdoor,' said Motley. 'In the good old days, they used to open it up and shove all the bad kids down here.'

'No they didn't,' I said.

'Yes they did,' said Motley, finishing his tea. 'Especially the ones that come disturbing people when they're hard at work.'

'Well that wouldn't be me then, would it?' I said.

So Motley went off to see what

Mrs T wanted, and I toddled along to class. And by the way, in case you're wondering, I really like Motley. I think he's brill.

The Interrupted Sausage

That night in our house we were all sitting round having tea late because little sister Tilly had been at ballet class and smelly brother James had been at football practice. There were a few chomping noises and a bit of slurping, then Dad

started off the same conversation that we always have every single night.

'So James,' said Dad. 'Good day at school?'

'Ur,' said James.

'So Tilly,' said Dad. 'Good day at school?'

'Ur,' said Tilly.

'So Agatha,' said Dad. 'Good day at . . .?'

WAM BAM BADDAM BAM!

I thought our front door was

going to explode.

'IT'S HIM!' shouted Ivy from outside. 'AGATHA, it's him!'

I ran to open the door before she broke it down.

'Now!' said Ivy. 'Quick.'

She grabbed my hand and yanked me down the path, out of our gate, into her gate and through the door of number 7.

'It's HIM!' she said pointing at the telly.

Gosh! She was right. It *was* him.

The man in his skinny black jeans and dark glasses was being interviewed by Grin Sickly. (He's the presenter with hair like a mouldy cycle helmet.)

'And where will the Zombie Bird appear?' Grin was asking him.

Ivy looked at me. 'What's a Zombie Bird?' she asked. I had no idea.

'The Zombie Bird will appear at the place chosen by the Pen of Destiny!' said Misto. He pointed down at a table where a fancy looking pen was lying on a big black cloth.

'AWESOME,' said Ivy.

'Take the pen,' commanded Misto. 'Reach under the cloth where nobody can see and draw a big cross on the table.'

So Grin fumbled about under the cloth doing as he was told, then

he pulled his hands out again. 'Done it,' he said.

'So be it!' said Misto. 'The Pen of Destiny has spoken.'

He took his pen back, then asked Grin to pull the cloth away. Underneath was a map, and we could see a blotchy red cross near the middle.

'Sorry, it's a bit messy,' said Grin.

'It is of no matter,' said Misto. 'For that is where the Zombie Bird shall be reborn!'

Slowly the camera zoomed in on the red cross. All the streets on the map got bigger and bigger until . . .

'It's ODD STREET!' yelped Ivy. 'The Pen of Destiny has picked our street! Oh **WOW!**'

She looked at me and then pulled a puzzled face. 'Agatha, there's something really bothering me,' she said.

'Me too,' I said. 'What was he doing in our school this morning,

when the pen has only just told him where to go?'

'That's not it,' said Ivy shaking her head. 'What I want to know is: why are you holding a fork with a sausage on it?'

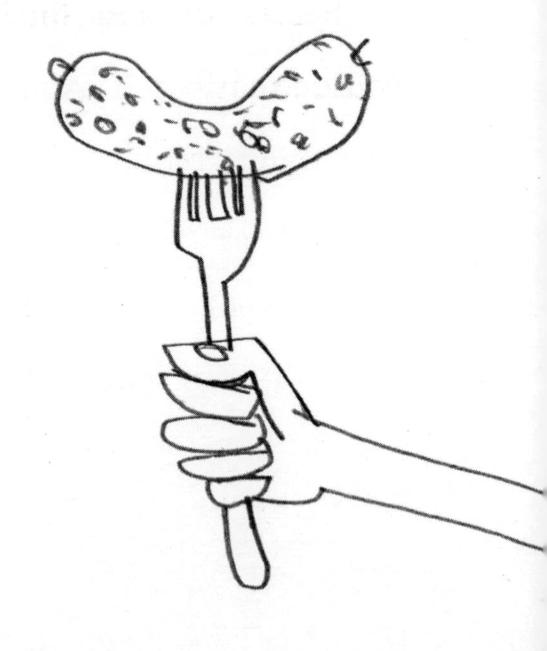

It's true, I was. **Wicked!**

Ivy had completely forgotten she'd dragged me away from eating my tea, and I didn't tell her. I bet she lay awake all night thinking I can do sausage magic **ha ha!**

Serves her right for interrupting sausage eating.

The Man With Moo Taps

Next day at school, we were all sitting on the bench in the playground apart from Ivy who was standing on one leg being a flamingo. It turned out that lots of people had seen the same telly programme, but only

one person had been impressed.

'It was the scariest thing I've EVER seen!' said Ellie. 'I had a bad dream last night that a big red pen was coming down out of the sky and going to squash me!'

Poor Ellie. She's always a bit nervous about things. One thing was for certain though, Misto must have known all along that the red cross was going to land on our school.

'But how could Misto be sure that

Grin would mark the right place?' said Ivy. 'He couldn't see through the cloth.'

'He must have moo taps,' said Bianca.

'*Moo taps?*' repeated everybody.

We love Bianca. Don't always understand her but love her. Try again Bianca.

'Moo taps!' she insisted. 'And he swapped them over.'

'She means TWO MAPS!' I said.

'That's it!' said Ivy the flamingo. 'Grin put a cross on one, but then Misto swapped it with another map that he'd marked himself.'

Oooh! Ah! Er? Hmmm . . . no.

We all had a big think about it, but the problem was that Misto never touched the map or the cloth. He couldn't have swapped them.

'Then the pen must be really magic,' said Ellie who was still

shivering with fear.

'No way!' said Martha. 'They sell those pens in my mum's shop.' Martha's mum works in Spendless which sells stuff you've never heard of. 'They look smart but they're all dried up and never work.'

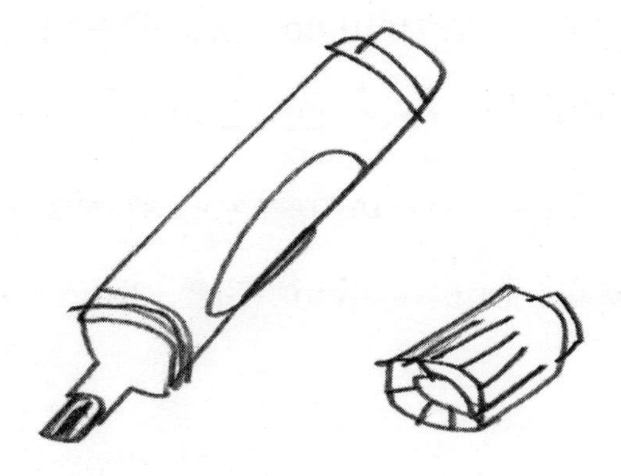

It didn't make sense at all. What was this Zombie Bird all about, and why was Misto coming to our school?

Ivy was still on one leg. Olivia Livid came charging up and pushed her over because that's what Olivia does. You don't want to know her. She's horrible.

'Go away Olivia,' said Martha. 'Or else . . .'

Martha was twice as big as Olivia, but Olivia just laughed.

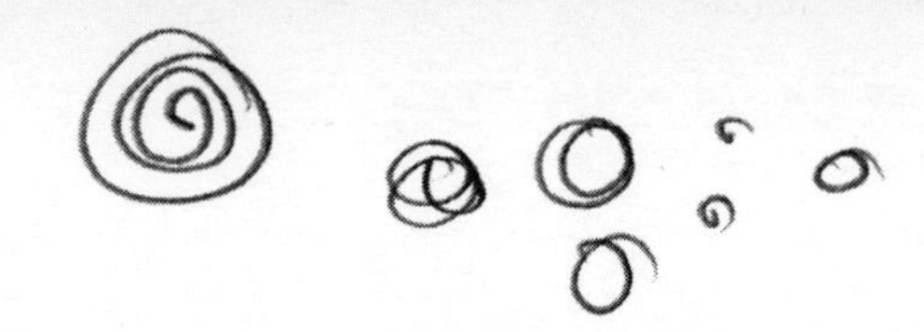

Everybody knew that lovely old Martha wouldn't ever fight anybody (apart from boys of course).

'Or else what?' said Olivia.

'Or else . . .' said Martha but she couldn't think of anything else.

But then Ellie jumped up and screamed, 'Or else a big red pen will come out of the sky and squash you!' and she pointed her finger right in Olivia's face and made her stagger backwards.

YO! GOOD ONE ELLIE! Shame that the pen thing was never going to happen.

'Oh, I get it,' said Olivia. 'You saw that magic man on the telly, didn't you? Well, guess what? Gwendoline actually knows him.'

By this time Gwendoline had turned up too. 'It was my dad who phoned up Mrs Twelvetrees and asked if Misto could come here,' she said proudly.

'Why?' we all asked.

'Because he was so good at my party,' said Gwendoline.

'So he IS Leggo Laughalot,' I said.

'He wasn't as good as the jellies,' said Martha.

'He's called Misto now,' said Gwendoline. 'And he needed somewhere to try out his new show, so I got Dad to arrange it.'

Ha ha! I bet Misto thought that Gwendoline's rich dad would

fix him up in the Grand Theatre or something. No wonder he was so grumpy when he came to look round Odd Street School!

'He's a rubbish magician anyway,' said Ivy. 'If he was any good, he could just magic himself a proper theatre up.'

'And how is he supposed to do that?' snapped Gwendoline.

'Like this!' said Ivy. She started leaping around waving her arms

and shouting, 'WAZZA DAZZA BINGO BONGO!'

Actually Ivy's spell went a bit wrong. She was making so much noise that all she magicked up was Miss Barking who told us to get into class. Gosh if Ivy ever learns to do real magic then I'm going to move to another planet.

Our first lesson was in the computer room. We LOVE the computer

room but our teacher Miss Pingle hates it. She's a new teacher and she's really nice and her hair changes colour every week. (This week's colour = Autumn Rose. Oooh, how super!) Poor Miss P is rubbish at computers, so that gave us the perfect chance to find out a bit more about the Zombie Bird. All I had to do was walk past the main computer and sneakily push a certain button . . .

'Now then children,' said Miss Pingle

when we were all sitting down. 'It's time to log on and put in your secret passwords.'

So we all logged on, and then we had to wait until Miss Pingle was ready with her computer at the front. Oh dear! She kept bashing away at the keyboard trying to put her secret password in, but it wasn't working. (Her secret password is her boyfriend's name d-a-v-e by the way so that's not very secret is it? Ha ha!)

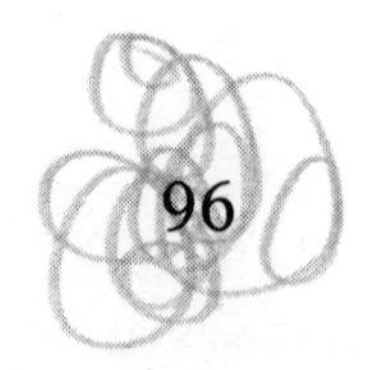

Click click click went Miss P on the keyboard, but I knew she'd never manage it. To be honest I felt a bit mean, but we had some important detective work to do.

We all got round Bianca who is a bit of a whizz at computers. She went on to the internet and typed in MISTO. A big picture of him in his dark glasses came up, and next to him was this giant bird with a head like a skull!

'WOW!' we all screamed.

'WHAT is going on in HERE?'

Oh potties. Miss Barking had arrived at the door and seen us all round Bianca's screen.

'Why aren't these children engaged in sensible computer activities, Miss Pingle?' demanded Miss Barking.

Poor Miss Pingle. She blushed a bit and gave her keyboard a last little prod. 'My password doesn't seem to be working,' she said.

Miss Barking stomped over and had a look. 'Somebody has pushed the CAPS LOCK button,' she said, and gave us all an evil stare. 'It makes everything into capital letters, so your password won't work.'

'Oh,' said Miss Pingle. 'I must have done it by accident.'

'Accident?' snapped Miss Barking. 'You shouldn't be in charge of a class if you're going to have accidents, Miss Pingle.'

Miss Barking gave us all another sniffy look then went off to go and bother somebody else. What a misery!

At least Miss Pingle wasn't a misery. She put her password in then she made a happy little squeaky noise like this: 'Oopy doo!' Then she pulled her serious teacher face and said, 'To your seats please, children. We're off!'

So we all got on with some computer stuff click click twiddle twiddle and that was that.

A Clue Full of Salad Cream

Thursday was a bit strange, because when we got to school, the playground gates were still locked. A big crowd of mums and pushchairs and kids had built up. Ivy wriggled her way through to the front and then pulled me and Martha after her.

Mr Twelvetrees was standing on the other side of the railings.

'Sorry,' he kept saying to everybody. 'Mr Motley is busy right now, but he'll open up as soon as he's ready.'

Across the playground we could see the black van parked on the forbidden space again. The van doors were open and Motley was carrying bags and bundles of stuff into school.

'What's all that lot for?' asked a mum.

'They're having a magician in today,' said another mum. 'I saw him on telly.'

'Oh really?' said the first mum. 'You'd think he could just wave his magic wand and get it all done a bit faster, wouldn't you?'

Everybody laughed including Mr Twelvetrees.

'This is taking ages,' said Martha.

'I'm dying of starvation out here.' She got a sandwich out of her bag and started eating it. 'Pickled onions and salad cream,' she said for anybody that was interested which actually was nobody. Yuk.

'Why are you here so early?' I asked Mr Twelvetrees.

'I came to help,' said Mr T. 'I've never had the chance to see a big magician get set up before.'

'So why did they make you

stand out here?' asked Ivy.

'I know,' I said. 'Mr Twelvetrees does magic. Misto doesn't want him to know how the Zombie Bird appears.'

Mr Twelvetrees turned to watch Motley, who was unloading a pile of black curtains. 'It's hardly a secret,' he muttered.

Eventually Motley shouted over from the main doors. 'You can open up now!'

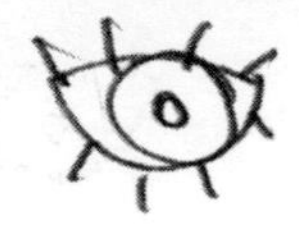

Mr T unbolted the gates and everybody poured through.

CHARGE!

Mr T got shoved against the wall by a river of mums, pushchairs, toddlers, bikes, random musical instruments and shopping bags. We went to rescue him.

'If it isn't a secret, can you tell us?' I asked him.

'Sorry,' he said. 'It's the rules of being a magician.'

'Aw!' said Ivy. 'Then give us a clue. Pleeeeeeeease?'

'Oh very well,' said Mr T. 'Martha's holding it.'

A sandwich?

Mr T winked. That was as much as he was going to tell us, but could we work it out?

Out of Bounds

When it got to playtime, everybody went outside except for me and Martha. We still wanted to know what sandwiches had to do with anything, so we decided to sneak into the hall and have a look.

To get to our hall you have to go past Miss Wizzit on reception, but

when we got there Mrs Twelvetrees was already standing by the desk with Misto.

'Everything is ready for our guest,' said Mrs Twelvetrees excitedly.

'Izzit?' said Miss Wizzit.

'Indeed it is!' said Mrs T. 'But now he needs to do a practice on his own, so could you see that nobody goes through the hall?'

'And that means NOBODY,' said Misto. 'Understand?'

Miss Wizzit grabbed a loose chair and plonked it down in the middle of the corridor to block the hall off.

'Thank you Miss Wizzit,' said Mrs T, and she went into her office.

Misto set off to go into the hall, but Miss Wizzit wasn't finished. 'Ex-CUSE me!' she called after him, pointing out of her window. 'What about that van. Are you going to move it?'

But Misto had already gone.

Miss Wizzit angrily snatched up her big stapler and quickly banged about ten staples all in the same bit of paper. Oooh, she was in a mood!

So far Martha and me had kept well back.

'How are we going to get past her?' asked Martha.

'There's only one thing for it,' I told her. 'We'll have to be invisible.'

How to Be Invisible

A lot of books get this SO wrong, so let's sort it out straight away. **NEVER** wear a magic invisible cloak. Everybody walks into you or sits on you, or if you're standing in front of the kitchen drawer when they need a teaspoon,

they suddenly reach out and grab you. And of course, if you put the cloak down somewhere you'll never find it. And if you're a bit smelly like you've just eaten a bag of chilli crisps or you're a boy or something, then people will know exactly where you are anyway. So NO INVISIBLE CLOAKS. Got that?

The real trick to being invisible is making sure that nobody actually wants to see you. For this story

Martha and me used a two-person method called The Measuring Project. Here's what you need:

- A ruler
- A calculator
- A pencil and paper

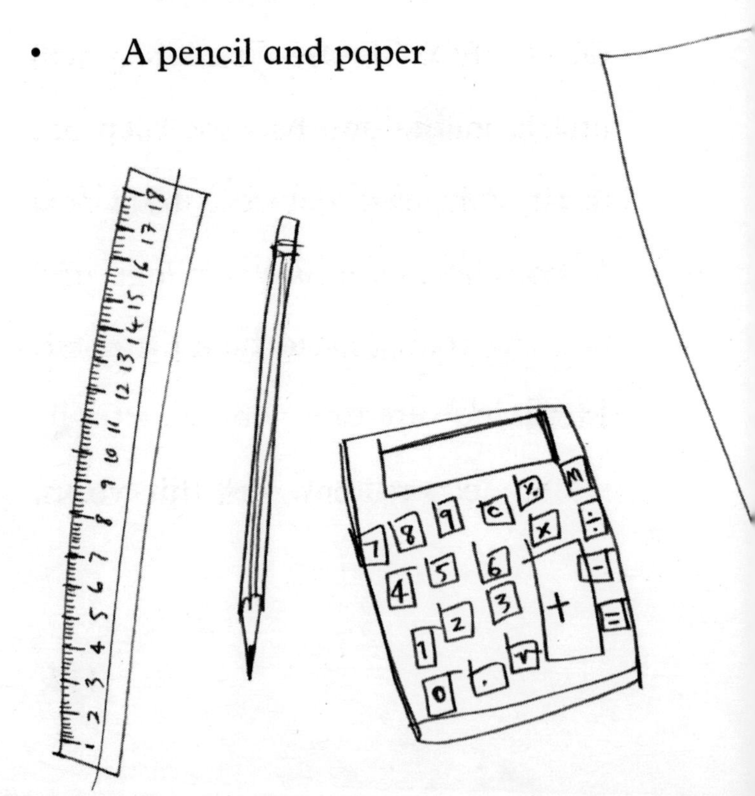

One of you creeps along the floor with the ruler looking very serious. The other one prods the calculator and writes down lots of numbers or draws a graph. If any of the OLD PEOPLE see you, they will utterly ignore you because they are terrified in case you ask them how to convert metres into gallons and how to put the answer on a pie chart.

Ha ha!

You can tell how well this works.

Look around you. Can you see a girl in a red sweatshirt with crazy hair and stunningly beautiful freckles (even though I say it myself)? No you can't. *But is there one there?* You will never know. Believe me.

When Martha and me tried it out, it worked perfectly.

We started on the far side of the reception area and slowly made our way along the wall. Martha was doing the measuring and I was making up the sums. Miss Wizzit was staring at some papers on her desk and it wasn't until we got to the chair blocking the corridor that she gave us a funny look. I prodded the calculator and said to Martha, 'Hmmm . . . I make it twenty-seven point six times a quarter metres squared, wouldn't you agree?'

'I'm not sure,' said Martha. 'Do you think Miss Wizzit would know?'

'Let's ask her,' I said.

Miss Wizzit immediately marched off into the office and shut the door.

Ha ha! We were in.

The Curtain Sandwich

It was quite dark in the hall. All the window blinds had been pulled down and two spotlights were pointing at a great big black curtain that was hanging up at the far end. There was some more black cloth on the floor in front of it. Somebody was

moving around behind the curtain, so me and Martha didn't dare go any closer. We just hid behind the plinky plonk piano.

Misto stepped out from behind the curtain. He fiddled with something hidden in the cloths on the floor, then he stood up and stamped his foot on it. It must have been a secret button because EEEKY FREAK there was a bright flash and suddenly there was a huge bird sitting on a perch in

front of the black curtain. Honestly, one second it wasn't there, and the next second . . . there it was!

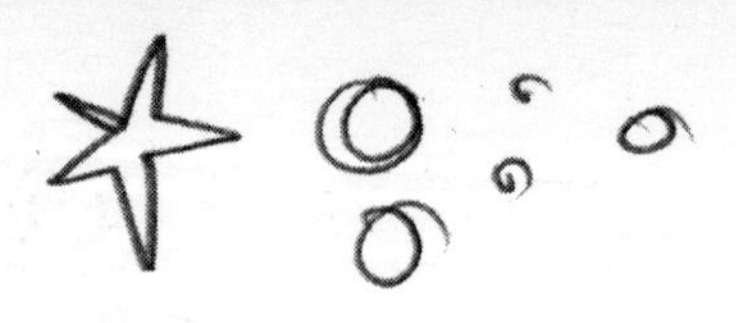

Its wings were a shiny blue colour, with bright orange tips on the end, and it had a really cross looking face. It was obvious that it wasn't real, but even so, me and Martha were both shaking.

'How did he do that?' whispered Martha.

'Mr Twelvetrees said it was something to do with your sandwich,' I whispered back.

'It was pickled onions and salad

cream,' nodded Martha. 'Maybe that's the secret?'

Hmmm. I'm sure pickled onion and salad cream sandwiches can do some strange things, but making Zombie Birds appear isn't one of them.

We thought the bird wasn't going to do any more, but then Misto went up to it and he waved his hands in its face. The bird opened its wings right up and it was MASSIVE like an aeroplane. The whole thing went

mad with the head swaying about and the beak snapping away and everything. AWESOME!

When Misto stopped waving, the bird's wings folded away and it went back to how it was. Misto pulled on a rope at the side of the curtains and a black cloth came up from the floor in front of the bird. The cloth was like another black curtain so when it got up to the top, the bird was completely hidden.

'So that's how it works!' I said. 'The curtain and the cloth are like a sandwich with the bird in the middle. When he stamps on the button the lights flash so that you don't see the cloth dropping down. All you see is the bird. '

'That's pathetic,' said Martha. 'Hardly magic at all.'

'Maybe, but I want to know how that bird works,' I said. 'We need to get closer.'

Martha stretched up to look over the top of the piano.

Plink!

Oh no, she'd knocked one of the piano notes. It was only a teeny little plink but it seemed to echo round the hall for ages. Misto immediately looked our way. We'd already ducked down again but we could hear him walking towards us. Argh panic panic!

But then we heard a little laugh come out of the middle of nowhere. Misto stopped walking. He'd heard it too! He looked round suspiciously

and then we heard the laugh again. It had come from somewhere at the far end of the hall. Misto walked back. Martha and me looked at each other. The laugh had sounded like an old man. It was dead spooky!

Misto was staring at the floor by his curtains. There was a very faint sound of music coming out, and then another laugh. I suddenly realised – it was Motley, and he was downstairs watching his secret telly!

'Let's go,' I said and pulled Martha to the doorway. 'Quick, while he's not looking.'

'But I thought you wanted a closer look,' said Martha.

'I do!' I said. 'But I've got a better plan. Come on.'

A Bit of Who Does What?

Lunchtime was good. Normally we have to have it inside, but because Misto had blocked up the hall and the corridor, they let us sit out in the playground. I was explaining to Martha and Ellie and Ivy and Bianca what they all had to do.

'But what if we get caught?' asked Ellie.

'You'll be fine Ellie,' I said. 'You're our lookout. If anybody comes, you just do a big cough and run off.'

'A big cough?' said Ellie. 'You mean like this? *A-hrumph!*'

To be honest it sounded more like Pukey with his head in the bucket, but Ellie didn't find these things easy.

'That's very good Ellie,' I said.

'A-hrumph!' went Ellie again proudly. 'This is THE most exciting thing I've EVER done in my WHOLE LIFE! *A-hrumph!'*

'OK, now Bianca,' I said. 'You know what you have to do?'

'I have to tray my plumbone,' said Bianca.

'Eh?' we all said.

'She means PLAY her TROMbone,' laughed Martha.

'That's it Bianca,' I said. 'And

you have to play it by the piano because you're waiting for the teacher. Got that?'

Bianca nodded.

By now Ivy was hopping up and down like crazy. 'What about me and Martha?' asked Ivy. 'What do we do?'

'We're all going to tidy the storeroom for Motley,' I said.

'WHAT?' protested Ivy. 'Boring boring with double extra boring on top.'

Martha calmed her down. 'It's

just part of Agatha's secret plan,' she said.

'A SECRET PLAN!' said Ivy. 'I LOVE secrets. What what what? Tell me.'

Thanks to Mrs Big Mouth Ivy a lot of people were staring at us, and then it got worse.

'A-hrumph!' went Ellie. *'A-HRUMPH!'*

'That's enough Ellie,' I said.

'No, I mean it!' said Ellie starting

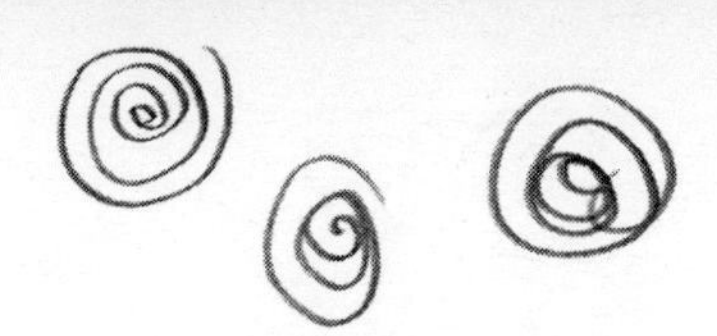

to panic. *'A-HRUMPH!'* Ellie pointed over my shoulder. Eeek! It was Miss Barking coming towards us. Ellie was about to run off.

'You girls, stay there!' ordered Miss Barking. 'I've got a few questions for you.'

Oh no! Had she heard Ivy shouting about the secret plan? Or maybe she'd found my fingerprints on Miss Pingle's CAPS LOCK key just like the police do on telly.

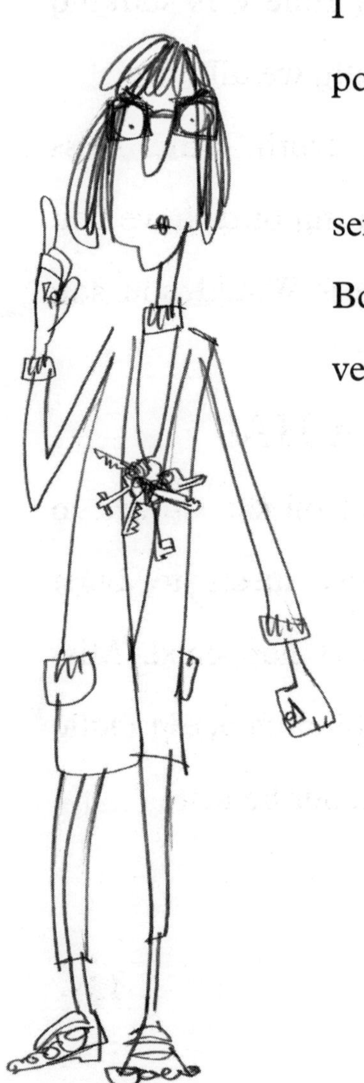

I wouldn't put it past her.

'This is very serious,' said Miss Barking in her very serious voice.

Oh boy. Poor Ellie was shaking like a jelly. Actually we all were.

'Tell me the truth,' said Miss Barking. 'How many birds have you seen on the feeder? Would you say *over one hundred?*'

HA HA HA HA!

Phew! Is that all she wanted to ask us? We didn't mean to burst out laughing, it just happened. Miss Barking looked a bit miffed, especially when we all shook our heads.

'*Over fifty* then? Or maybe *over twenty-five . . .*?'

It didn't take her long to realise that she couldn't tick any boxes on her bird food form, so off she went. Bye bye Miss B thank goodness.

We cleared our bits of lunchtime rubbish up and took it over to where Motley was standing by the lunch bin.

'Finished already?' asked Motley.

'We only wanted a snick quack,' explained Bianca, then she ran off to

get her trombone.

Motley watched her go. 'A *snick quack*?' he repeated.

'QUICK SNACK,' we all said.

'Oh,' said Motley. 'What's the rush?'

'We're going to tidy up the store room for you,' I said.

'Tidy the store room?' said Motley. 'No way. I'm not letting you lot in there. You're not allowed.'

'Why not?' I said. 'We'd be glad

to help. After all, you're always so busy! You've got the bins to empty, chairs to put out, drains to unblock, *telly to watch . . .*'

'Telly?' gulped Motley.

'Has he really got a telly?' said Ellie.

'Shhh!' said Motley looking round nervously.

'Telly telly telly telly telly,' said Ivy. 'TELLY.'

'Please!' said Motley. 'Can you

shut her up somehow?'

'Hmmm . . .' I said. 'If only there was somewhere nice and quiet that we could take her?'

'How about the store room?' said Martha.

'Oh, now that IS good thinking!' I said. 'Well, Mr Motley?'

Ha ha! Poor old Motley. What choice did he have?

Bwarb Barp Bwab

The others had never been down to the store room before. It is completely **brilliant**. There's some top hats, a gold mirror, about 300 different wings for fairies, angels, bats, butterflies and . . .

'. . . goblin ears!' said Ivy.

Sure enough she'd found a headband with two huge pointed ears stuck to the sides.

'Try them on, Agatha!' said Ivy.

'No way,' I said. 'We've got work to do.'

'Go on,' insisted Martha. 'You'll look great.'

'No.'

But Martha moves fast for a big person, and next thing I knew she'd grabbed me, and Ivy and Ellie had jammed the ears on my head.

'When you've quite finished . . .' I said, but I couldn't help having a look in the mirror.

'HA HA HA HA!' we all went but then, '*Shhh!*'

There was a noise coming from just above us.

CLUMP CLOMP CLACK!

We were standing under the trapdoor, and we could hear Misto

walking about guarding the hall.

'Get ready everybody,' I whispered. 'Bianca should be there soon.'

Sure enough, a few seconds later we heard a great big *BWARB* noise from upstairs. It was Bianca's trombone.

'You can't come in here!' shouted Misto, and we heard his feet clump clomp clacking down to the far end of the hall.

Ellie slipped out of the store room door and up to the top of the stairs to be the lookout. Me and Martha and Ivy pulled a table across then put a chair on top. I climbed up and pushed on the trapdoor.

'It's heavy!' I said, so Martha climbed up on the chair too and we both pushed. It moved, just enough for us to peer out.

It was really dark. We were right at the end of the hall behind the black curtains where Misto had piled up all his bags and boxes. We could hear Misto and Bianca down at the other end of the hall.

'Get out!' Misto was saying. 'Go on, go now.'

'But I've got to tray my plumbone!'

BWARB BARP BWAB!

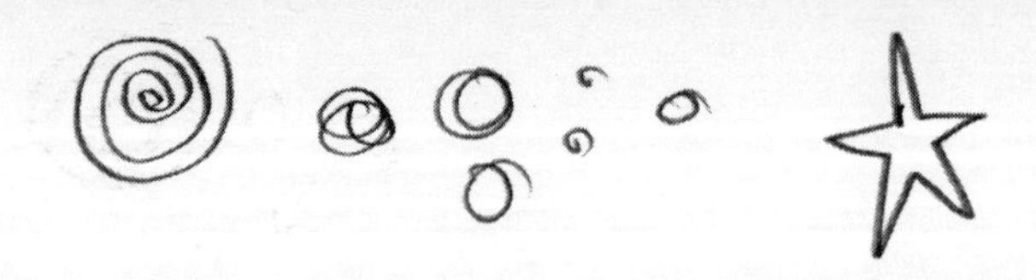

Martha and me pushed harder on the trapdoor so it opened right up.

'Go on, I can hold it!' said Martha who's dead strong. That must be what pickled onion and salad cream sandwiches do for you.

I managed to wiggle my way up, and the next thing I knew, Ivy had come up too. We stood behind the curtains and held our breaths and listened.

'You can't be in here!' Misto was saying.

'But I'm laiting for a wesson,' said Bianca.

'Eh?' said Misto.

'And I need to scoo my dales.'

BABB BABB BABB BABB BABB BABB BABB BABB . . .

(In case you hadn't worked it out, she was doing her scales which is like the most boring tune you can play. It's guaranteed to drive anybody nuts. Ha ha wicked! Good one Bianca.)

Me and Ivy were standing in front of a window. Although the blind was down, it gave us enough light to find the gap in the middle of Misto's black curtains. We opened them up a tiny bit. Just as I thought, the black cloth was hanging down on the other side, so if Misto turned round, he wouldn't have seen us. We opened the curtains a bit more and there, on a stand with its back to us, was the big bird!

'Oh wow!' hissed Ivy. 'Is it real?'

'No,' I said. 'Of course not.'

And that's when it turned its head right round to look at us. EEEKY FREAK!

I nearly screamed, but then I realised there was nothing to scream about. The bird wasn't scary at all, it just looked old and tired. Two sad eyes were watching us, probably waiting to see if we were going to wave in its face. When the bird

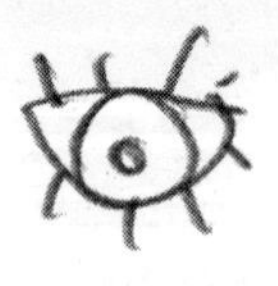

realised we weren't going to scare it, it tipped its head over and looked at us sideways, so me and Ivy tipped our heads sideways too. It seemed like good manners.

(I don't know why birds tip their heads sideways when they look at you. Maybe it's a sort of bird joke and they like to pretend to themselves that you are walking up a wall. I tried looking at Miss Pingle sideways once to see if it

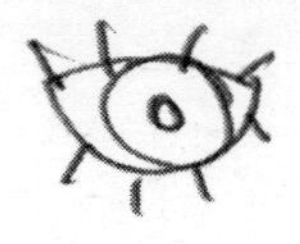

worked, and actually, if you give it a few seconds it's quite funny. **WAHOO** bird jokes! We love them.)

'The poor thing's shivering,' I whispered. 'And it's been painted to make it look like a zombie. This isn't right.'

'We ought to go and tell Miss Barking,' said Ivy.

'We can't!' I said. 'We're not supposed to be here.'

'We have to do something,' said Ivy. 'You're pulling your hair.'

She was right. That's what I always do when I'm thinking of something. It wakes my brain up.

Meanwhile, at the far end of the hall, Misto was still trapped by Bianca.

BARB BARB BWARB!

'Stop it little girl! You must go. NOW!'

'But I've got to get teddy for the reacher,' said Bianca.

'You mean you're getting ready for the teacher?' asked Misto.

'Yes,' explained Bianca patiently. 'She does the poosick on the miano.'

BWARRRBBBB.

The bird was still giving me a funny sideways look, so I sneaked a bit closer. There was a metal ring around its leg, and looped through it was a chain holding the bird on to the perch. No wonder the bird didn't fly away when Misto waved at it! The chain ran down the back of the stand and was hooked round a nail at the bottom.

The bird lifted its foot and rattled

the chain, then gave me another sideways look. Ooh! Suddenly it was obvious what I had to do.

Just then there was a scuffle noise behind me. Ivy had got her shoe tangled up in a black wire and unplugged it from something.

'Put it back!' I whispered.

But then Martha started waving at us. From far away I could hear *a-hrumph* so I dived back through the trapdoor.

'Come on Ivy!' I hissed. But Ivy had crawled off to plug the wire back in. Martha and me could hear grown-up footsteps already coming down the stairs into the store room. We had no choice! We shut the trapdoor and jumped down off the table and tried to look normal . . . but looking normal isn't easy when you suddenly remember that you've got giant goblin ears.

EEEK!

'They've been very helpful,' said Motley's voice.

'Have they really?' said a voice that I DIDN'T want to hear!

Motley and Miss Barking were just stepping in through the door as Martha yanked the ears off my head.

'Agatha! Martha!' snapped Miss B. 'The store room is out of bounds. Mr Motley is supposed to keep it locked.'

'Don't blame Mr Motley,' I said. 'He asked us to find something to use as a bird table.'

'Did I?' asked Motley.

'Oh yes,' I said. 'You thought it would be helpful for Miss Barking's bird project.'

'Did he?' asked Miss Barking.

'Of course!' I told them. 'It was going to be a nice surprise for you Miss Barking, but now you've found us, you've spoilt it.'

'Have I?' said Miss Barking.

'What a pity,' I said. 'But it wasn't your fault Miss Barking, you weren't to know. Don't blame her, Mr Motley.'

Motley looked at Miss Barking in a confused way. 'I'm not blaming you,' he said.

'Thank you,' said Miss Barking who was even more confused than Motley.

'Well, we can't stay here chatting

or we'll be late for lessons,' I said. 'And you know how we HATE to get into trouble . . .'

. . . And half a second later me and Martha had escaped up the stairs and run into the cloakroom. We knew Ellie would be there hiding behind the coats, and sure enough we could see her little knees sticking out underneath and wobbling with fear.

'It's OK, Ellie!' said Martha.

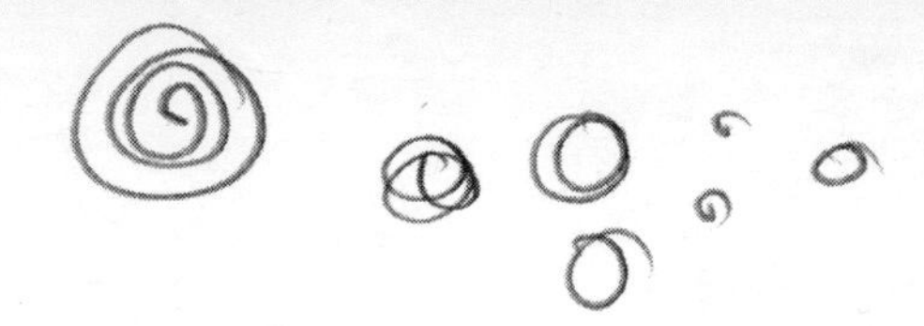

'You can come out.'

The coats opened up a tiny bit and Ellie's face peered out. 'How how did you get away from Miss Barking?' she asked.

'Agatha was just her usual brilliant self,' said Martha.

What a nice thing to say! True of course. But still nice.

Martha and Ellie went back to class, but I had to get Bianca. I went to reception and found that Misto

had come out of the hall to argue with Miss Wizzit.

'Why didn't you stop that girl going into the hall?' he demanded.

'I'm busy,' said Miss Wizzit who was STILL staring out of the window.

'Busy? Doing what?' demanded Misto.

'Busy waiting for that van to be moved,' said Miss Wizzit.

BWARB BAB BWARP came

echoing down the corridor. Misto clenched his teeth and jammed his fingers in his ears which made his dark glasses fall off. I picked them up and passed them back.

'Here you are,' I said to Misto. He had really piggy little eyes ha ha! 'Can I go in and talk to my friend?'

'Yes yes yes!' said Mr Piggy Eyes. 'Just get her out of there.'

Misto followed me into the hall. Bianca was taking a deep breath for another mighty blow.

BWARR-WARR-WARR!

'Hey Bianca,' I said. 'You can stop now. The teacher's not coming.'

'Why not?' asked Bianca.

'She can't get her car in. Some idiot has parked a van in the way.'

'What a milly san,' said Bianca. Then she pointed her trombone at Misto and gave him one final *BWARB*. 'Bye bye,' she said politely and off she toddled.

Misto slumped into a chair and held his head in his hands. No wonder. He'd just been completely and totally Bianca-ed. I almost felt sorry for him, but then I remembered that poor bird stuck in the dark between the curtains.

Ho ho! Misto might have thought Bianca was bad, but that was just for starters.

Before we get to the next chapter, I know what you're thinking. What

was I going to do about Ivy?

The answer to that is a big fat **NOTHING.**

We left her stuck behind the black curtains at the end of the hall, remember? It might sound bad but in Ivy world, it's no big deal. She's always doing mad stuff like getting lost in big shops or losing her shoe down the toilet. One time when we were all on holiday she managed to get herself locked inside an ice cream van! It was a bit brilliant actually because she tried to climb out of the sun roof and accidentally snapped off the ice cream tap and it all started to squirt out everywhere **ha ha** . . . oh sorry. The old man who is typing this book out for me says we're running out of pages so I have to finish this story about the Zombie Bird first.

The Tremendously Exciting But Quite Long Chapter

(If you haven't got enough time to read this chapter all in one go, I've marked the halfway place so you can do it in two bits.)

By the time Bianca and me got to class, everybody was lined up by the door ready to go to the

hall. Miss Pingle was as excited as anybody else, and she hadn't noticed that Ivy wasn't there.

The door opened and Mrs Twelvetrees was standing outside being all excited too.

'Are you ready for this, chaps?' she said with her necklaces all jangling. 'Isn't it thrilling? Now would you like to make your way to the hall . . .'

WAHOO! CHARGE!

WHIZZ! THUNDEROUS POUNDING OF FEET!

'. . . slowly and quietly.'

By the time she'd finished talking there was nobody left in the classroom. In fact I don't even know if Mrs T did say the 'slowly and quietly' bit because I'd already gone too. But she probably did say it because that's the sort of thing headteachers always have to say even though nobody ever listens.

Bless her for trying, eh?

I have to admit it, the hall looked really good because Misto had got lots of flashy lights going. There was some music playing too, and all the tiddly tots at the front were bouncing on their bottoms in time to it bumpy-dumpy-dump.

Once we were all in, Mrs T got up at the front. The music went off and all the tiddly tots went 'booo!' and started picking their noses.

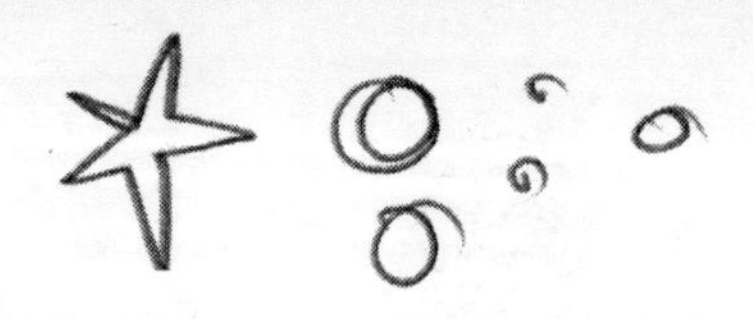

Mrs T did the usual speech that headteachers always do for visitors. 'We're very fortunate . . . *blah blah waffle* . . . very special guest . . . *bit more waffle* . . . very best behaviour . . . *yawn! Is she STILL talking?* . . . so let's give a very warm Odd Street welcome to MISTO THE MYSTERIOUS!'

Everybody clapped, then there was a big flash right behind Mrs T.

'WHOOPS!' she giggled, and

hurried off to the side to watch.

Misto walked on in his dark glasses. A few of the tiddly tots said, 'Hello' and, 'Why are you wearing those funny glasses?' and, 'Do you think it's sunny in here?'

'Shhh!' said Miss Bunn reaching over and tapping them on their heads.

Misto started with some small tricks. First he did the one where the blue cloth goes into a top hat and

comes out yellow. Next he did the one where the metal rings all link up, and then that other one where the rope gets cut and it glues itself back together again. We must have seen them about a billion times before, but for one of us it was still magic.

'Did you see that?' gasped Ellie clutching my arm. 'Oh, that is just so amazing!'

Good for Ellie! She was absolutely loving it until Misto reached into a bag and pulled out . . .

'The PEN of DESTINY!'

Misto announced it with a big boomy voice.

'Oh . . . ooh!' said Ellie trying not to be frightened.

'I need a helper, but who shall it be?' said Misto.

Loads of people put their hands up including Miss Pingle.

'The pen shall decide!' said Misto.

'Oh no, please not me!' said Ellie.

I don't know why she was worried. We all knew EXACTLY who it was going to be. Gwendoline's hair had been done up with pink streaks and glitter spray, and she even had sparkly tights on.

Misto held up a folded sheet of paper. 'A list of every child in this school,' he said.

Misto then asked Mrs Twelvetrees to come up. She had to hold the paper behind her back so nobody could see

it, and unfold it. Next she had to take the pen and reach behind and put a tiny cross on the paper.

'Can you feel the magic of the pen?' asked Misto.

'Oh gosh, jolly rather!' said Mrs T.

Misto took the pen back then asked her to look at the paper. 'What name has the pen chosen?'

Mrs T held up the paper so we could all see there was just one little red cross on it. She adjusted her glasses then peered at the name. She took a deep breath. Big excitement . . . *NOT.*

'It's Gwendoline Tutt!' said Mrs Twelvetrees.

Gwendoline marched up the front and did a big girlie curtsey to Misto. **YUK!** In fact it was so YUK that a strange gurgle noise came from the end of the row where we were sitting. It was Pukey Higginson's stomach.

Smoke
MACHINE

Misto put a golden crown on Gwendoline's head.

'You are the beautiful princess,' said Misto.

Gwendoline did such a smug smile, Pukey couldn't take it any more. He ran out to reception to stick his head in a bucket and I don't blame him.

Misto showed Gwendoline where to stand, then stepped back to a little desk and pushed some buttons. The lights flickered and there was a blast of big music:

BARHHH – DUM DUM DUM – BA-BARHHH!

'Wooo!' went the tiddlies.

'Golly!' said Mrs T.

Misto then gave Gwendoline what looked like a red shoe box.

DUMMY DUM BASH went the music.

'It is your sixteenth birthday, and you have been given a mysterious gift!'

Gwendoline sniffed at the box and was about to open it, but Misto stopped her.

'Oh no, princess! This gift is enchanted, you must not open it until midnight! You must place it on the table.'

Misto pointed at a little table just in front of the curtains. Gwendoline put the box on it.

'You must now stand back and wait,' he said. He made Gwendoline

hold her hands out towards the box as if it was going to do something exciting.

'The palace clock chimed twelve,' said Misto.

BONG BONG BONG BONG BONG etc.

(Yes I know there's only five BONGS, but the old man who's typing this book out couldn't be bothered to do them all. You'll just have to read them twice and then do two more for luck. And yes that DOES make twelve BONGS because I tested it for you because I'm nice like that.)

(Oh, and you're exactly **halfway** through the chapter now if you want to stop for a rest.)

After the last BONG Misto waved his hands at the box in a magic way. It opened all on its own and the sides fell down. (I *wish* I knew how it did that. Honestly, for me it

was the best bit.) Left sitting there was a big shiny egg.

'The princess thought the silver egg was a rare jewel,' said Misto. As he talked I spotted his foot feeling around for that pedal thing hidden under the cloth!

'But it was a TRAP! The silver egg had never been laid by a goose or a hen. NO! This egg had been dug from a graveyard. And at midnight it turned into the . . .'

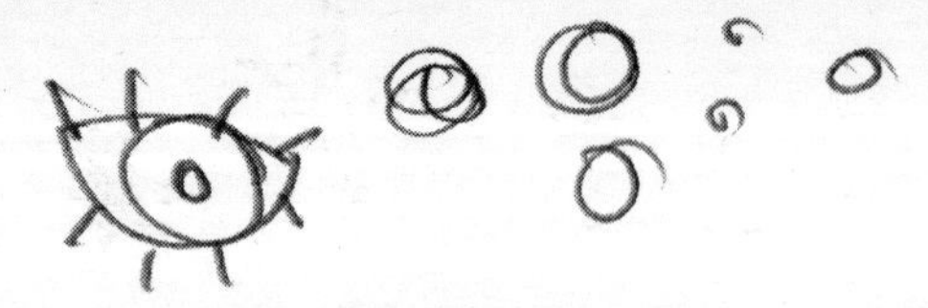

Misto did a big wave of his arms and stamped his foot down.

'. . . ZOMBIE BIRD!'

FLASH went all the lights, and a big blast of smoke went up. It was totally awesome, apart from one tiny little detail.

'Where's the bird?' shouted the tiddlies.

Misto stood there looking like he'd been slapped with a sausage. He waved his arms and stamped his foot

again, but still . . . no bird!

That's when I remembered the wire that Ivy had pulled out behind the curtains. It must have been the wire that was supposed to make the cloth drop. I bet she never plugged it back in. Whoops!

Misto did one more magic wave of his arms, then ran round the back of the curtains to see what was wrong.

'He'll see Ivy!' hissed Martha.

'No,' I said. 'Even Ivy's got the

sense to hide herself.'

It had all gone very quiet. Everybody started to giggle a bit because the only thing left to watch was Gwendoline. She was still standing there on her own with her hands pointing at the egg looking silly **ha ha!**

Gwendoline was getting really embarrassed. She was just about to storm off when suddenly . . . **PLOP!** The black cloth fell down

and the bird appeared.

Of course that was supposed to be the big exciting moment, but the best bit was that the cloth had landed right on Gwendoline's head so she disappeared! Maybe we were supposed to clap but everybody (including the bird) was too busy watching Gwendoline trying to fight her way out of the cloth and in the end she fell over.

HA HA HA HA HA!

Misto ran back. ‘It’s the ZOMBIE BIRD!’ he shouted. ‘Don’t be frightened little ones!’

Frightened? Who was he kidding? Everyone was laughing themselves silly. Misto did a big angry snarl at the audience, then waved his hands in the bird’s face.

‘SCREEEECHHHHH!’ went the bird and it opened its wings right up.

‘ARGHHH!’ went everybody. Tremble tremble panic panic. Even

me and Martha were a bit freaked, and we'd seen it before!

'HAR HAR!' shouted Misto. 'I am the ONLY person who can control the Zombie Bird!'

He waved his hands in the bird's face again. The bird reached its wings out and stretched up higher and higher . . . and then the chain dropped off its leg. (Gosh how did that happen I wonder? Tum-tee-tum, don't look at me.) The bird rose right up into the air.

'Oo-er!' said Misto looking shocked.

The bird did a full circle round the hall, then it swooped down, glided over the heads of the tiddlies and went to sit on the radiator.

'Come back here!' shouted Misto. He was doing some magic hand waving, trying to pretend it was all part of the show. 'Misto the Mysterious commands you!'

But the bird wasn't impressed so Misto had to go and get it. He took one step then fell over a big black

Gwendoline-shaped lump that was rolling about on the floor. The bird tipped its head sideways and stuck its tongue out.

HA HA HA HA HA!

Misto got up and ran towards the radiator. The bird waited until he got close, then it took off again and landed on the top of the climbing bars.

Misto climbed up after it. He tried to grab the bird's leg, but it fluttered over on to one of the ceiling lights. Misto fell off and landed on the piano

KA-CHINK-A-PLONK!

'Oh, he is SO funny!' hooted Mrs Twelvetrees and everybody gave him a nice round of applause clappy clap clap.

I've got to be fair here. Misto was putting on a brilliant show. The tiddlies were totally rolling about with laughter, in fact everybody was. We were all a bit sad when

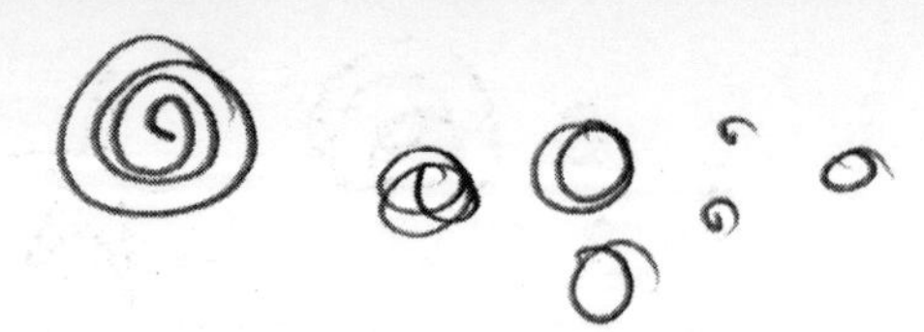

the bird flapped across the hall and disappeared behind the black curtain. A big disappointed 'AW' noise went up, but we didn't know the best bit was still to come!

Misto went stomping over and pulled the curtain right back. He was expecting to see the bird but there was no sign of it!

'EH . . . ?' gasped Misto.

'Oh look, children,' said Miss Bunn. 'The Zombie Bird has

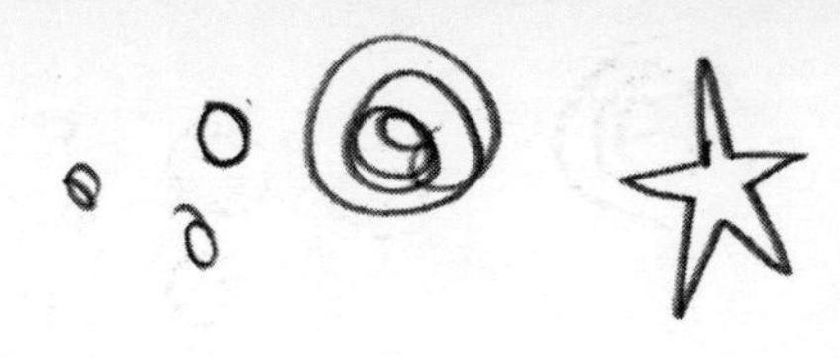

magically disappeared! Isn't that clever?'

And that's when Gwendoline finally managed to crawl out from under the cloths. She stood up with her hair looking like the Zombie Bird's nest, and her face was as cross as a squished tomato.

'And the beautiful princess lived happily ever after,' said Miss Bunn.

'Hooray!' cheered all the tiddlies.

All Misto could do was pretend to smile and bow while everybody clapped. And then, just to finish it off nicely, while he was bending over, Gwendoline ran up and gave him a whacking great big kick on the bottom.

Lovely.

Ellie the Witch!

After school we were all outside round Misto's van. Mr Twelvetrees had been helping Misto carry his stuff out.

'Oh go on!' we begged Misto. 'Tell us how the bird disappeared! PLEEEEEEEEEASE!'

SLAM SLAM went the back

doors, as Misto finally finished loading everything up.

'No!' he snapped.

(Ha ha! Of course we were just winding him up. He had no idea what had happened to the bird – but we did! When the bird flew behind the curtains, Ivy was climbing out of the window. The bird shoved its way out past her and off it went. Then Ivy closed the window behind her and slid down the drainpipe. Easy really.)

Misto marched round to the driver's door but Martha was leaning against it so he couldn't get in. She's good at leaning against things is Martha, because there's a lot of Martha to lean.

'Go on, tell them how you did it,' chuckled Mr Twelvetrees. 'Or they'll never let you go!'

Misto muttered crossly. 'I can't. I'm a magician. It's against the rules.'

'Ah, the rules!' said Mr Twelvetrees.

'I'm glad you mentioned the rules. What would the Magicians' Council say if I told them how you treated your bird?'

'What bird?' said Misto. 'I haven't got a bird!'

'Not now, you haven't,' said Mr T. 'But don't think of getting another one. I don't want to hear any more about Misto the Mysterious.'

'You'll have to go back to being Leggo Laughalot,' I said.

'Don't call me that,' snapped Misto.

'Then what shall we call you?' I asked. 'I know – let's ask the Pen of Destiny.'

'I've lost it,' said Misto

'Don't worry,' said Martha. 'We've got one! Show him Ellie.'

Ellie reached into her bag and nervously pulled out one of the big pens from Martha's mum's shop. She held it out along with a folded piece

of newspaper. 'Hold these behind your back please,' she said to Misto.

Misto tried to ignore her, but Mr Twelvetrees smiled nicely.

'Go on! Or shall I phone the Magicians' Council?'

Misto snatched the paper and pen.

'Open up the paper and draw three little circles on it without looking,' said Ellie.

Misto had no choice.

'And now,' said Ellie proudly, 'the Pen of Destiny will tell us what to call you!'

Misto brought the paper out from behind his back. There were hundreds of words on it, but only three of them had inky circles round them!

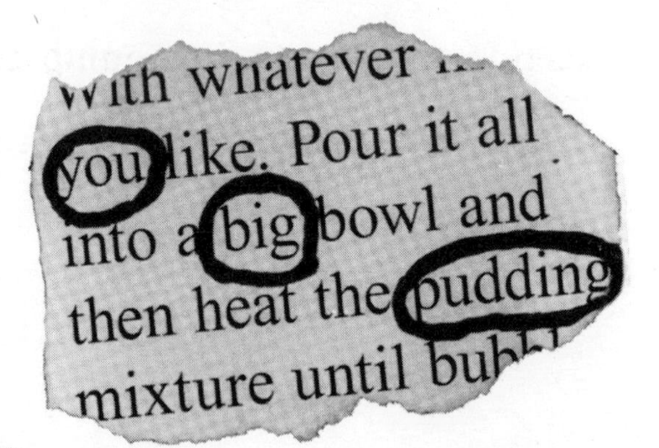

YAHOO! GOOD ONE ELLIE!

Do you know how Ellie did it? There is a clue on page 87 if you want to have a look. If you still don't get it then I'll tell you at the end. Promise promise.

But first I've another promise to keep. I said at the beginning there would be some *real* magic . . . and here it comes!

A Bit of *REAL* Magic!

It was the morning after the show, and we were all in the playground. Miss Barking came out to check the bird feeder. It was a bit sad really. She stared at the tubes really closely, but she couldn't kid

herself. They were all completely full to the top.

She was just about to give up and go away when there was a big flapping noise. A great big bird came down and perched next to the feeder.

We all recognised it straight away because it still had some paint on its wings! It looked nervous so we backed away to give it a bit of space. Only Miss Barking stayed where she was.

After a while she fished a couple of bits of food from the feeder and held them out in her hand. The bird looked at her and she looked at it . . . and then it bent down and started pecking at the food. When it had finished, it hopped over to the feeder and got stuck into the rest.

AT LAST Miss Barking could tick some boxes on her bird form! Then she reached up and gave the bird a little stroke, and guess what? For the first time ever in the whole of history, Miss Barking SMILED! Let's have a big clap for Miss Barking. Well actually not too big, we don't want to scare the bird away, so just fingertip clapping

. . . tippy tip tip.

Now that's what I call *real* magic!

The Ending

There, that's the end. I was going to tell you all about Ivy getting stuck in the ice cream van but we've already used too many pages so the printer people will be getting cross. Sorry about that! We'll just have to have a very quick finish so thanks very much for reading this

book LOVE YOU LOTS WAHOO and GOOD BYEEEEE!

Oh potties. I just remembered about the extra end bit I promised you, so we'll have to squeeze it in. The old bloke that types this out is muttering that he'll be the one that gets into trouble with the grumpy printers but that's HIS problem ha ha! Here we go . . .

How the Pen of Destiny Works

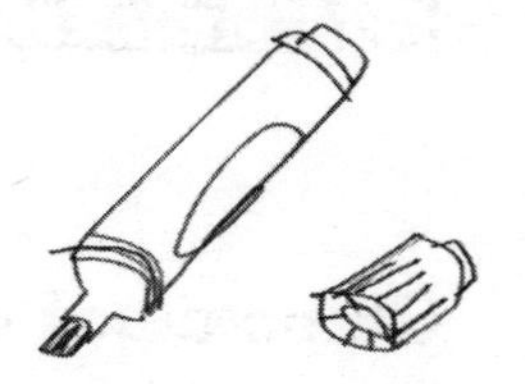

(We found out from Mr Twelvetrees so a big THANK YOU to him!)

Did you find the clue on page 87? It's when Martha says 'the pens never work.' That's the secret!

If you want to do the trick, you get your map or piece of paper or

whatever it is, and you get a working pen and mark the paper where you want before you start. You then fold it up or cover it with a cloth so nobody can see you've marked it. Then you pass over a pen that doesn't work! The person has to mark the paper without looking, but of course it doesn't make a mark at all. When they see your mark later on, they'll think they did it.

TA-DAH!

Look out for

and the Floating Head

Hiya! This book is about Odd Street School where I go with mad Ivy who always jumps down stairs four at a time WAHOO! And Martha who is big and can sort out boys anytime.

The oddest teacher we've got is Miss Barking who wears goggles and gloves to use a pencil sharpener. This story is about when she tried to execute Martha with a floppy cardboard axe, but instead Martha's head floated off and exploded ha ha brilliant!

Agatha Parrot

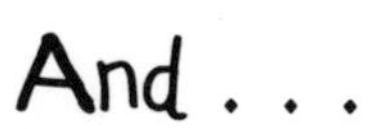

And . . . Agatha Parrot and the Mushroom Boy

Helloooo! This story is about the time I was watching SING, WIGGLE AND SHINE on TV (the worst talent show ever WAHOO love it love it) but my evil brother James nicked the TV remote so he could watch football instead. Don't worry, I got my own back!

All it took was a giant yellow cake, some fairies, a school fete and a big sofa cushion. Oh, and Dad ended up with his toenails painted, so does that all make sense to you? It will do when you've read this book ha ha wicked!

Agatha Parrot

EGMONT PRESS: ETHICAL PUBLISHING

Egmont Press is about turning writers into successful authors and children into passionate readers – producing books that enrich and entertain. As a responsible children's publisher, we go even further, considering the world in which our consumers are growing up.

Safety First
Naturally, all of our books meet legal safety requirements. But we go further than this; every book with play value is tested to the highest standards – if it fails, it's back to the drawing-board.

Made Fairly
We are working to ensure that the workers involved in our supply chain – the people that make our books – are treated with fairness and respect.

Responsible Forestry
We are committed to ensuring all our papers come from environmentally and socially responsible forest sources.

For more information, please visit our website at www.egmont.co.uk/ethical

Egmont is passionate about helping to preserve the world's remaining ancient forests. We only use paper from legal and sustainable forest sources, so we know where every single tree comes from that goes into every paper that makes up every book.

This book is made from paper certified by the Forestry Stewardship Council (FSC®), an organisation dedicated to promoting responsible management of forest resources. For more information on the FSC, please visit **www.fsc.org**. To learn more about Egmont's sustainable paper policy, please visit **www.egmont.co.uk/ethical**.